This book belongs to

. . . .

. . . .

For Tim, who gave me the idea
— D. B.

Published by
PEACHTREE PUBLISHERS
1700 Chattahoochee Avenue
Atlanta, Georgia 30318-2112
www.peachtree-online.com

First published by Oxford University Press in Great Britain in 2004
First US edition published by Peachtree Publishers in 2004
First trade paperback edition published in 2015

10 9 8 7 6 5 4 3 2 1 (hardcover)
10 9 8 7 6 5 4 3 2 1 (trade paperback)

Printed in April 2015 in China

Library of Congress Cataloging-in-Publication Data:

Bedford, David, 1969-
    The copy crocs / written by David Bedford ; illustrated by Emily Bolam.— 1st ed.
        p. cm.
    Summary: Annoyed when the other crocodiles crowd and copy him, a young croc goes off
by himself, only to find that he sometimes enjoys the company around him.
    ISBN 978-1-56145-304-7 (hardcover)
    ISBN 978-1-56145-885-1 (trade paperback)
    [1. Crocodiles—Fiction. 2. Friendship—Fiction.] I. Bolam, Emily, ill. II. Title.
PZ7.B3817995 Co 2004
    [E]—dc22   2003016531

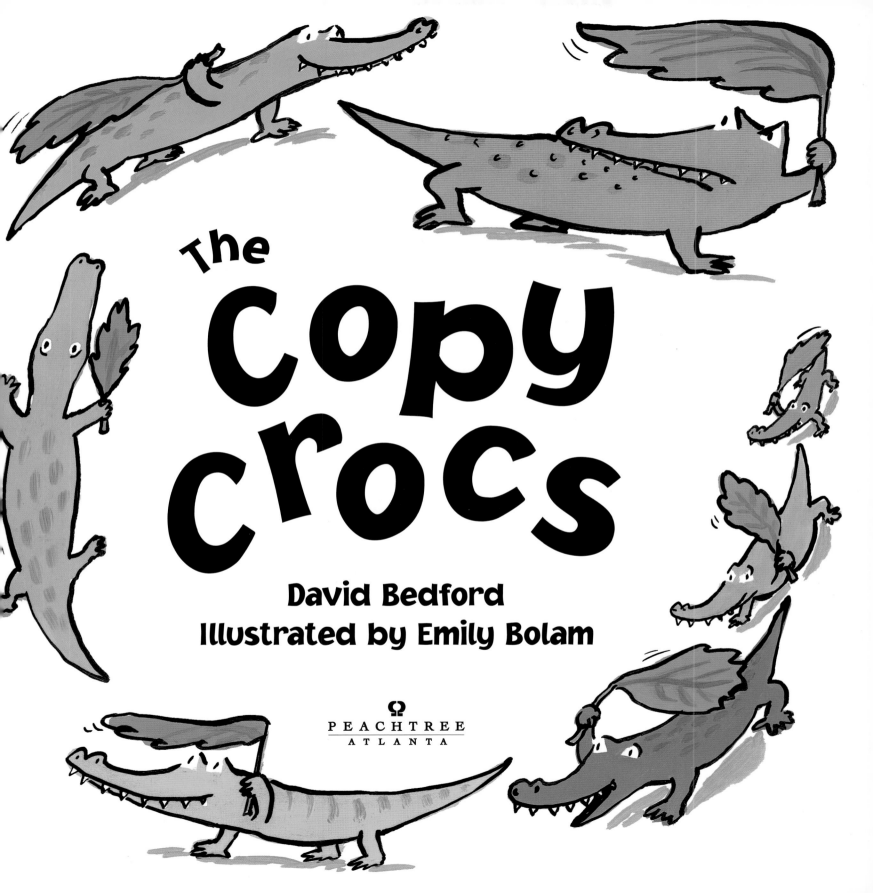

The Copy Crocs

David Bedford

Illustrated by Emily Bolam

PEACHTREE
ATLANTA

Crocodile had always lived
in the same pool and he liked it.
But he didn't like sharing it with all the other crocs.
Every time Crocodile moved, he bashed into someone.
And when the other crocs moved, they bashed him back.

"Stop pushing!" Crocodile shouted.
"You stop pushing!" said the other crocs.
It was too crowded, so Crocodile crawled out of his pool
and went to find somewhere else to live.

Crocodile found a new pool that was filled with slippery mud.

He liked it.

He really enjoyed sliding and rolling about.

But when the other crocs saw what Crocodile was doing…

…they started sliding and rolling about too.
"Stop copying me!" shouted Crocodile.
But the crocs said, "We can slide and roll
if we want to. It's not your pool."
Crocodile was so angry that he jumped
out of his muddy pool and ran away.

Crocodile found a place by the river
and stretched out in the sunshine.

He liked sunbathing.

But when he fell asleep…

...the other crocs came and sunbathed too!
It was so crowded that Crocodile could hardly move.
He was furious.
"Leave me alone!" he shouted.

Then he slipped into the cold river and swam away.

Crocodile found a floating log. He climbed on top of it,
kicked his feet, and glided down the river.
He liked watching the frogs and birds.

And he liked being on his own.

But then he heard a splashing sound and…

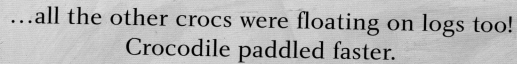
...all the other crocs were floating on logs too!
Crocodile paddled faster.
When he passed a bend in the river, he hid behind some bushes.
The copy crocs were having such a good time that they didn't see him.

Crocodile crept through the jungle until he
saw a mountain sitting all on its own.
"That's my kind of mountain!" said Crocodile.

He started to climb.

At the top of the mountain,
there was only room for one crocodile.

Crocodile was happy.

But when the sun went down and it was getting dark...

…all the other crocs squeezed together
on Crocodile's mountain too!
"Why do you keep copying me?" Crocodile shouted.
"Because you're always doing new, fun things,"
said the other crocs. "Anyway, we can sit here if we want.
It's not your mountain."

Crocodile
waited until
the other crocs
were sleeping. Then
he crept silently away…

...back to his pool.
Crocodile swam about
and didn't bash into anyone.
He never knew his pool was so big.

But Crocodile felt cold and lonely in the empty pool.
He remembered how it used to be packed with a
snug pile of snoring crocs.

"I wish my friends were here," said Crocodile sadly.

"SURPRISE!"
all the crocs shouted. "Here we are!"
They were laughing and bashing and rolling about.
Crocodile felt WONDERFUL.

He decided he did like sharing his pool
with the other crocs, even if
it was a bit of a squeeze.

But sometimes he liked to slip away…

...and do something
on his own,
before
his friends
found
out...

...and joined in too!